Little Mouse Grandma

Julia Jarman

Illustrated by **Alex de Wolf**

mammoth

Also in the **MAMMOTH STORYBOOK** series:

Blair the Winner! Theresa Breslin
Magic Betsey Malorie Blackman
Tricky Tricky Twins Kate Elizabeth Ernest
Oh, Omar! Lisa Bruce
Kamla and Kate Jamila Gavin
Connie and the Waterbabies Jacqueline Wilson

First published in Great Britain in 1997
by Mammoth, an imprint of Reed International Books Limited
Michelin House, 81 Fulham Road, London SW3 6RB

Text copyright © 1997 Julia Jarman
Illustrations copyright © 1997 Alex de Wolf

The rights of Julia Jarman and Alex de Wolf to be identified as the author and
illustrator of this work have been asserted by them in accordance with
the Copyright, Designs and Patents Act 1988

ISBN 0 7497 2822 1

10 9 8 7 6 5 4 3

A CIP catalogue record for this title
is available from the British Library

Printed and bound in Great Britain by
Caledonian International Book Manufacturing Ltd, Glasgow

Contents

~

Thank you to Gay Wilkinson
who told me she was
Little Mouse Grandma

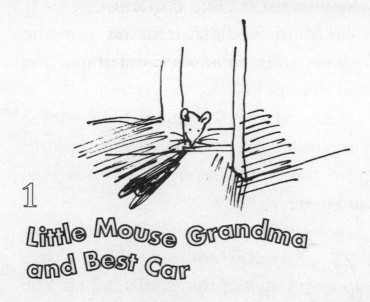

1

Little Mouse Grandma and Best Car

Only Matthew knew that his grandma was really a mouse! His mum didn't know. His dad didn't know. Nobody else knew. They knew Matthew called his grandma Little Mouse Grandma, but they didn't know why. Only Matthew knew that when the front door banged shut, and the car doors banged shut and his mum and dad's car rumbled down the drive into Ashdale Close – then his grandma turned into a mouse.

So Matthew didn't mind his grandma looking after him when his mum and dad went out.

'Little Mouse Grandma! Little Mouse Grandma! Are you coming upstairs now?' he would shout as soon as they had gone.

 'In a minute Matthew. I just want to put these dishes away,' she would call back in her ordinary grandma voice, because she was an ordinary grandma most of the time. She lived in Luddington Crescent in a bungalow.

Then Matthew would know she was in the kitchen in her ordinary clothes, looking sleek and trim and only a little bit mouse-like with her short grey hair and shiny brown eyes. He would hear the chink of cups as she stacked them tidily on the cupboard shelves. He would hear the cupboard doors snap shut.

Then he would hear nothing at all.

Because you can't hear a mouse, however hard you try, if you're sitting in bed at the top of a house and the mouse is two storeys below. You can't hear a mouse scampering across the kitchen floor and into the hall and up the stairs and across the landing. You can't hear mouse feet on carpet, even when the mouse is just outside your bedroom door. But you can see one if your door is open.

You see her shadow first, a big mouse shadow, on the landing wall – and that's scary, till you see a small mouse nose poking round the door and whiskers trembling as the mouse leans against the door frame.

She's puffing a bit because it's a long, long climb up thirteen steps and then seven more to the top of the house.

'Little Mouse Grandma, is that really you?' Matthew always asked when he saw her, just in case an ordinary mouse had just happened to peep into his bedroom.

'Yes Matthew, it's me.' Her mouse voice was more a whisper than a squeak.

'Then come in, Little Mouse Grandma.'

And she would come running in, on all four paws, across the wooden floor. She'd stop and sit up on her grey haunches, and look all around, listening. She would run and stop, and stop and run, till she was on his bedside mat, looking up at him with her bright-bead eyes. Then he would lean over and pick her up very gently, and she would sit on his hand, and he would gaze at every tiny bit of her. Her grey-brown velvet back, her pale honey-coloured tummy, her dainty paws with their tiny nails and pink pads, her silver whiskers.

And then they would decide what to do.

One Sunday evening his mum and dad went out to dinner at Mr and Mrs Scantlebury's. Matthew hadn't been invited so he waved goodbye from his bedroom window, then he shouted, 'Little Mouse Grandma!'

And there was a clink and a thud from downstairs, as if someone was closing the knife drawer.

'Little Mouse Grandma!' Matthew shouted again. Then he heard the hoover. Little Mouse Grandma was very tidy, but Matthew knew she'd be up to see him as soon as she'd tidied downstairs.

Matthew looked at his bedroom. It wasn't very tidy, so he got out of bed and put his bricks in his brick box. He put some Lego in his Lego box and some books on his bookshelf. Then he picked up his dungarees – and he saw Best Car!

'Best Car! I've been looking for you everywhere!'

This wasn't quite true, but he had missed Best Car a lot. It was blue with yellow wheels.

'Brrrrrrm.' He raced the little car across the bedroom floor. Bumpff! There wasn't much room for racing. There were too many things in the way. His room was still rather untidy. Matthew sat Ted on the bed and he started to pile up his comics. Then he lifted up a dinosaur jigsaw — and he found his garage! And some more cars! So he made a race track with lots of dangerous bends and he put all his cars in a line. Then he raced them.

'Brrrrrrm!' went the red racing car.

'Brrrrrrm!' went his fire engine.

'Vrrrrrrm!' went his Batmobile.

'Whooosh!' went Best Car!

Best car was fastest. It went past the red car, past the fire engine, past the

Batmobile and under the bed.

Matthew didn't like under-the-bed.

He knew what was there – a mat that should have been beside his bed, some socks, some paper, some Lego, a water pistol, which Mum didn't like him to play with, a little pile of toenails and some dust. Mum didn't like hoovering as much as Grandma did.

He knew what was under under-the-bed. Dad had shown him when he lifted the floorboards to put a radiator in Matthew's room. There were pipes and wires and wooden joists and more dust. There was nothing to be frightened of. But he was frightened. It was partly because it was dark under the bed and partly because of what his cousin Jemma

had said. She had made a joke once —
about dead men and dust. He didn't
understand it, but he couldn't forget the
joke. It was creepy.

So there he was, sitting on the bedroom
floor, wishing he was brave enough to
get Best Car, when he felt something
tickling his hand: whiskers! And paws —
and a pointed nose that never stopped
moving!

'Little Mouse Grandma!' He had
forgotten about her.

She ran up his finger-ramp, and
on to the back of his hand.
'What's the matter
Matthew?'

'It's Best Car, Little Mouse Grandma.
It's gone under the bed.'

Little Mouse Grandma wasn't afraid
of under-the-bed. She wasn't afraid of
dust or dark, though she said light would

be better for looking. She asked Matthew to lie on the floor and hold his bedside lamp like a searchlight. And he did. He couldn't see Best Car, but he could see lots of things that he hadn't remembered losing – a dice, a twenty-pence piece and a bar of toffee, wrapped, so it wasn't dusty. There were springs too, bed springs. You could see them if you looked up through a hole in the material that covered them. Little Mouse Grandma said springs made the bed bouncy. Matthew liked bouncing.

But he didn't bounce now. He was too busy holding the lamp, so that Little Mouse Grandma could run to and fro under the bed looking for Best Car. He tilted it up when she climbed up – inside one of the springs, till Matthew could see only her tail. He pointed it down when she came down – head first.

Unfortunately she said she couldn't see Best Car. So Matthew swept the searchlight from left to right and back again, but he couldn't see it either.

'I think it's gone down a hole, Little Mouse Grandma.'

There was a hole in the floorboards close to the wall.

'I shall go and investigate,' she said, and Little Mouse Grandma whisked down the hole, under under-the-bed.

Matthew couldn't hear a thing.

Then he thought he could hear some squeaking, even some huffing and puffing and a knock and a clatter. In fact there was a lot of squeaking and

huffing and puffing and – the number plate of Best Car! BC 1! There it was, coming out of the hole! Then it wasn't. There was a clatter as it disappeared.

Then there was more squeaking and huffing and puffing. There it was again, BC1! And so were the bonnet and the yellow front wheels of Best Car – which looked as if they were going to roll back again. But with a squeak, several squeaks, then a long, loud squeak which sounded very much like, '*Heeeave!*' the front wheels didn't roll back. They rolled forward and the back wheels followed!

Best Car, pushed by five little mice, came out of the hole.

Then Little Mouse Grandma came out of the hole too. She climbed into Best Car and started to drive it!

Matthew moved to one side as she drove out from beneath the bed and then round the race track twice.

'There you are, Matthew. Now into bed with you,' she said as she stepped out of the car. She was very dusty. So was Best Car. Matthew dusted it with a sock and Little Mouse Grandma flicked fluff off her tail. 'I must go and wash and change now. I can't let your mum and dad see me looking like this, can I?'

Matthew got into bed, with Best Car of course. He found his lion hot-water bottle cover and he put the tufty tail against his nose as he always did. Then he snuggled down. He could hear Little Mouse Grandma in the bathroom next door, and he felt very safe and sleepy.

2

Little Mouse Grandma and Mr Yaffle

One Saturday morning, when Matthew came downstairs for breakfast, his mum was wearing a pink hat. 'We're going to the races, Matthew,' she said.

'Oh good. I like races,' Matthew replied.

'Sorry, Matthew. These races are for grown-ups,' his mum said.

Then his dad came in from the garden. He was wearing his best suit –

with a rose in the buttonhole
and he said, 'Sorry, old man.'
That's what he called
Matthew – old man.

'Can't I watch the races?'
Matthew asked. But his mum said they
were going to watch horses racing and
little boys weren't allowed.

Matthew was disappointed. Even
when his mum said Little Mouse
Grandma was coming round to look
after him, he was still disappointed. He
wanted to see horses racing. He'd seen
them on the telly. They went very fast
and sometimes they jumped over fences.

Little Mouse Grandma arrived just
after breakfast – as an ordinary
grandma. She wore grey corduroy
trousers and a blue anorak and a red
safety helmet, because she'd come on her
bike. She was a bit puffed. She said there

was a head wind blowing.

Matthew's mum said, 'I'm sorry I didn't have time to do the dishes, Gran.'

And his dad said, 'Wish us luck, Gran!' as he pulled Matthew's mum out of the door. Then Mum waved as the car whooshed down the drive.

Matthew didn't wave back. He told Little Mouse Grandma about wanting to see the horses racing.

She said, 'I can't do anything about that Matthew, but I'm sure we can have an interesting day. I'll clear the dishes and think about it. You think about it too.'

So, while Little Mouse Grandma was clearing the dishes, Matthew went into the garden to think.

He thought about climbing his climbing frame.

Then he thought about climbing the

ash tree at the bottom of the garden.
His mum said he could when he was
older. The tree had two grey trunks,
which formed a big V near the bottom
that Matthew liked to sit in – so he did.

Matthew looked up at the blue sky.
He could see a lot of sky because it was
spring and there weren't many leaves on
the branches. He could see clouds
scudding by, ever so fast, as if they were
racing. One cloud looked like a poodle
dog, and the poodle-dog cloud was
racing a crocodile cloud, and the
crocodile was racing a big fish cloud,
and the big fish was racing a
little fish.

It was a blowy day and the tree swayed and creaked a bit. Most of the branches had thick black buds, shaped like crayons, and he was thinking about doing some crayoning when he heard a strange whirring noise. What could it be?

At first he thought it was Little Mouse Grandma in the kitchen, mixing a cake with the electric mixer, but then he realised that the noise was coming from above. So he looked up and saw a flash – a yellow-green bird flash! He could see that it was a bird, though he couldn't see its head because it was moving so fast. Then it stopped and he could see its head, its red head, and something landed on Matthew's nose. And as he brushed it off, the yellow, green and red bird flew out of the tree and over the fence into the garden next door.

What had it been doing, making such a noise? Matthew peered into the branches. Then he stood up and grasped a sturdy branch above his head. He saw a little ledge where he thought his foot might fit – and it did. So he pulled himself up, and there was another sturdy branch waiting for him to grasp it.

He was climbing – and it was wonderful!

Stretch – pull – stretch!

Stretch – pull – stretch!

As he climbed higher it got darker because there were even more branches and twigs and leaves, but he wasn't frightened, not a bit. He felt like a prince fighting his way through the forest – to a hidden castle.

Stretch – pull – stretch!

Stretch – pull – stretch!

Then he was there – in the light again – right at the top! King of the castle!

Close to the poodle clouds chasing each other across the sky. Close to the tops of other trees which looked like a pile of colourful cushions. Some were covered with pink blossom, some with bright green leaves.

He was close to the roof tiles of the red brick houses in Ashdale Close. He could see a pigeon on the chimney pot of his own house. 'Coo, coo,' it throbbed.

It thinks I'm a pigeon, thought Matthew. Perhaps I look like a pigeon in my blue-grey dungarees.

Then he looked down and saw the garden far below.

He saw his climbing frame. He saw the grass and the flowerbeds and his trike and his sandpit. And he saw the kitchen door opening, and he thought he saw Little Mouse Grandma. She looked tiny.

'Little Mouse Grandma!' he yelled, and the pigeon flew off the chimney pot.

'Little Mouse Grandma!' he yelled again in his loudest voice, and the branch swayed.

'Little Mouse Grandma!' He really did want her to hear him and see him. He wanted to wave, but the branch was swaying quite a lot and the wind was whooshing through his hair, so he held the branch tightly with both hands.

Suddenly he wanted to be *near* Little Mouse Grandma. He wished he could be sure that she had seen him.

He looked down again, but the grass below wobbled and he felt a bit sick. Now he longed to be at the bottom of the tree. So he crouched a bit, and started to lower himself. But it was harder going down than up. You had to stretch your leg down to find a foothold, then let go with your arm for a second and grab the branch again lower down.

It was stretch – let go – grab – stretch – let go – grab, and the letting go was scary.

It was even scarier when he *didn't* go down, when he stretched his leg and couldn't go any further, when he couldn't move because something was holding him back. And all round him the branches were creaking and swishing even more because it was getting windier. What could he do?

He looked around – not all around – because he couldn't turn round either. He looked up, to where he could see some patches of blue sky, and he looked down, to where he could see the back door, and he yelled: 'HELP! HELP! LITTLE MOUSE GRANDMA! I'M UP THE TREE AND I'M STUCK! HELP!'

But there wasn't any answer.

He couldn't see whether she had heard or not.

He couldn't see because you can't see a mouse, however hard you try, if you're in the middle of a tree and the mouse is far below in the grass, and the grass is tall with clover and daisies growing in it.

You can't see a mouse and you can't hear her.

So you don't know whether anyone is coming to help you or not. You don't know if you'll be stuck in a tree all day long, till night comes.

You just don't know.

Matthew didn't know how long he had been there waiting and waiting, wondering if Little Mouse Grandma was going to rescue him, when he felt something touching his hand – and there she was!

'Little Mouse Grandma! I'm so glad to see you!'

She didn't say anything at first. She was a bit puffed,

because it's a long way from the
back door, through the grass and
up the trunk and along the branches to
the top of a very tall ash tree. And as
Little Mouse Grandma sat on Matthew's
hand, which was gripping the branch
very tightly – her pale honey-coloured
tummy went in and out very quickly.

'Are you all right, Little Mouse
Grandma?'

'Of course I'm all right,' she said at
last. 'Now let's see to you.' She ran up his
arm – it tickled a bit – and on to his
shoulder.

'The strap of your dungarees is
hooked over a branch,' she said. 'I'll have
to chew off the button.' Then she
disappeared down his back, but after a
few minutes he felt looser – and she was
on his shoulder again. 'You can climb
down now,' she said.

It wasn't so scary with Little Mouse Grandma by his side guiding him and pointing out interesting things, like the woodpecker's hole. That's what Matthew had heard. The yellow, green and red bird was a woodpecker. It must have been drilling into the tree.

'I felt something land on my head,' said Matthew.

'Sawdust,' said Little Mouse Grandma. 'Or a chip of wood.'

'Can I see inside?' he asked.

'We'd better ask Mr Yaffle,' she said. That's what she called the woodpecker who landed beside them. She talked to the woodpecker – in a strange language, which sounded like laughter – and the woodpecker talked back!

Little Mouse Grandma told Matthew that he could look if he promised not to tell anyone, because Mr Yaffle had a secret. Matthew promised, then they both looked in the hole and there at the end of a sloping tunnel was Mrs Yaffle sitting on a nest of woodchips. She lifted a green wing to show six white eggs!

When they got to the bottom of the tree Matthew and Little Mouse Grandma were very hungry.

'You look for your button in the grass,' said Little Mouse Grandma, 'while I get lunch.'

3

Little Mouse Grandma and Ginger Biscuit

Little Mouse Grandma had a very good nose. It was very good at sniffing. Little Mouse Grandma always knew if Matthew had eaten anything after he had cleaned his teeth or just before his dinner. And she knew what he had eaten. She would say, 'Was that a strawberry-flavoured Chewit, Matthew?' or 'Have you had some cheese and onion crisps tonight?'

Little Mouse Grandma loved cheese and onion crisps. So did Matthew, and he always saved her one if he had a packet. He liked to see her nibble it, holding it in her paws. It took her thirty seconds to eat one crisp. He had timed her by his Tom and Jerry bedside clock.

Little Mouse Grandma didn't like his Tom and Jerry clock.

She didn't like cats.

So it was a bit of a shock one day when Matthew's mum said, 'We're going to have one of Pussy Willow's kittens, Matthew. You'll like that.'

Pussy Willow was Mrs Scantlebury's cat, and Matthew's mum had taken Matthew to see her. She was tabby and white, and very fat. She was fat because she was going to have

29

kittens. They were inside Pussy Willow right now, Mrs Scantlebury said.

'When they are born, you can have first choice, Matthew,' she said.

'I don't want one, thank you,' said Matthew.

But Mrs Scantlebury didn't seem to hear him. 'She'll have them any day now,' she continued.

'I don't want one,' Matthew said again.

'Oh you will when you see them,' said Mrs Scantlebury. 'I expect Pussy Willow will have at least three kittens. You'll be able to have one when they are seven weeks old.'

Matthew told Little Mouse Grandma about Pussy Willow's kittens the very next time she came. She was being an ordinary grandma that day because his mum was there. They were all in the kitchen.

'We're going to have one of her kittens,' he said, 'and it will grow into a cat.'

His mum laughed. 'Matthew's like you, Mum. He's a bit afraid of cats, but I'm sure he'll like his very own kitten, when he gets to know it.'

Matthew said, 'I'm not afraid. I just don't want one.' But his mum was busy taking a cheese pie out of the oven. She had made it specially for Little Mouse Grandma, who loved cheese even when she was an ordinary grandma. Cheese pie was her favourite.

When Little Mouse Grandma came upstairs to say goodnight, she told Matthew not to worry. 'I'm sure we shall manage,' she said. 'Kittens are small. They sleep a lot and they can be trained. Choose a small one.'

Pussy Willow had four kittens and Matthew chose the smallest. It was sleeping when he chose it. Matthew thought a sleepy kitten would be best. He called it Ginger Biscuit, because it looked like a ginger biscuit – round and golden-brown.

It slept all the way home in the car, in a wicker basket. But then it woke up and Matthew began to worry again because, when it wasn't a sleeping kitten, it was an exploring kitten with bright blue eyes. It was a boy kitten and a hunter.

Ginger Biscuit watched things . . . and leaped on them! He pounced on paper – including the newspaper when Matthew's dad was reading it! On shoe laces – whether anyone was in the shoes or not. On grass. On leaves. On anything. He hunted everything that moved and some things that didn't.

Matthew worried a lot.

His mum made two rules. GB – that's what they called Ginger Biscuit – wasn't allowed on the table and he wasn't allowed upstairs.

But Ginger Biscuit wasn't very good at rules.

If he jumped on the table, Matthew's mum or dad thwacked the table with a rolled-up newspaper, and Ginger Biscuit jumped off. But he climbed back again.

When they found him upstairs they shooed him downstairs. But he climbed back again.

He was so good at climbing! He climbed up the curtains and along the top of the curtain rail. And he made wild leaps – from the curtain rail to the dresser, from the dresser to the table. He was fearless.

Matthew kept his bedroom door closed. He was very worried. For a whole week Little Mouse Grandma hadn't come to visit. Matthew phoned her.

'Are you frightened, Little Mouse Grandma?'

'I'm apprehensive, Matthew.' (What did that mean?) 'But I'm coming tomorrow, when your mum and dad go to the cinema.'

'I shall put GB outside, Little Mouse Grandma.'

Matthew tried to as soon as she arrived. When he saw Little Mouse Grandma on the step, he carried Ginger

Biscuit to the door, and he was about to put him outside when his mum said, 'GB can't go out on his own, Matthew. He's only eight weeks old.' She closed the front door.

'But Little Mouse Grandma doesn't like cats.'

'You don't mind kittens, do you, Gran?' Matthew's mother asked.

'I'll manage I'm sure,' said Little Mouse Grandma.

Ginger Biscuit watched Little Mouse Grandma. He watched her from the stairs as she took her coat off. He watched her walk into the kitchen. Then he sat by the waste bin and watched her eat her tea. It was as if he was waiting for something.

'I don't know what's got into GB,' said Matthew's dad. 'I've never seen him so still.'

Little Mouse Grandma watched Ginger Biscuit.

When Matthew's mum and dad set off for the cinema they said, 'Make sure GB doesn't go upstairs, Gran.'

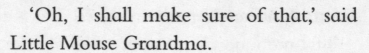

'Oh, I shall make sure of that,' said Little Mouse Grandma.

From his bedroom, Matthew heard the front door slam and the car doors slam. He saw the car lights backing into Ashdale Close — and he ran to his bedroom door.

'Little Mouse Grandma! Are you all right?'

'Yes, Matthew. I'm washing the dishes!'

He could hear the dishes clinking. She sounded just like an ordinary grandma and Matthew had a sad thought.

Perhaps she'd stay an ordinary grandma now, all the time, because that was safest?

'Little Mouse Grandma! Are you coming upstairs to play with me?'

'In a minute, Matthew! I'm drying the dishes!'

Listening hard, he heard the chink of cups and saucers, as she stacked them on the shelves. He heard the cupboard doors snap shut.

Then he heard nothing at all.

He watched his bedroom door. He waited for her shadow to appear on the landing wall. He waited for her tiny nose to poke round the door.

But it didn't. So he shouted: 'Little Mouse Grandma!'

Then he listened as hard as he could, but he couldn't hear anything.

'Little Mouse Grandma!'

Why didn't she answer him?

Matthew called again. Then he went downstairs — carefully, because he didn't want to tread on her if she was coming up.

But she wasn't on the first flight of steps.

She wasn't on the second flight.

She wasn't in the hall as far as he could see, but there was a grandfather clock there and a wooden chest and three open doors, so she could be hiding.

'Little Mouse Grandma!'

'Miaow!'

He saw Ginger Biscuit's tail – through the sitting-room door – swishing wildly, as it sometimes did just before he sprang.

'Little Mouse Grandma!' He ran into the room.

'Shush, Matthew.' She was a mouse – and she was standing on the coffee table, looking down on Ginger Biscuit.

He was in a fix, rolling from side to side, trying to unravel the wool wound round his body. But he was making it worse. For Ginger Biscuit was tied up – like a very tight parcel!

'Did you do that, Little Mouse Grandma?'

'Of course not, Matthew. GB is quite capable of getting into trouble without my help. He attacked your mother's knitting.'

'Mia-owwww!' Ginger Biscuit cried mournfully.

'I think the wool's hurting him, Little Mouse Grandma.' Matthew knelt down to look. Then he tried to undo the tangles and knots, but he couldn't get to them. Ginger Biscuit was in a frenzy, trying to free himself, but all he was doing was scratching and biting his own fur.

'Miaow!'

Oh dear. Matthew wasn't fond of Ginger Biscuit, but it was a sad thing to see him in distress.

Little Mouse Grandma wasn't fond of Ginger Biscuit, so what she did next really surprised Matthew.

She ran down the leg of the coffee table and across the carpet, till she stood right in front of Ginger Biscuit's mouth.

'Mia-ow!' he wailed.

Little Mouse Grandma looked straight into his blue eyes.

'Be quiet, GB,' she said firmly – and he was quiet. 'And be still,' she said – and he was still. Then she said, 'I want a promise from you.'

And when Ginger Biscuit had promised never, never to chase her, Little Mouse Grandma started to bite through the wool that was binding him.

It took her a whole hour but she let
Matthew stay up to watch.

Then she shooed him upstairs.

'I've got a bit of sorting out to do
before your mum and dad get back,' she
said.

But Matthew said, 'How do you know
GB will keep his promise?'

And Little Mouse Grandma said,
'Look at him.'

Ginger Biscuit was curled in front of
the fire, looking like – a ginger biscuit!
He didn't stir even when Little Mouse
Grandma stood on the rug and gently
pulled a whisker!

'Goodnight, Matthew,' said Little Mouse Grandma.

'Goodnight, Little Mouse Grandma,' said Matthew.

4

Little Mouse Grandma and the magic powder

Matthew had chicken pox. It was horrid. It covered him with scabby spots and he had them everywhere. They were on his hands and on his arms and on his legs and on his tummy. They were on his face and even in his hair – and they itched horribly. His mum said he mustn't scratch them – but he did sometimes, and that made them sore. So he felt sore and itchy and scratchy and cross, even though everybody was very kind to him.

He got lots of Get Well Soon cards.

He got lots of presents including a Corythosaurus from Miss Chatt next door, who was collecting dinosaurs for him. She got them free with packets of tea.

He got all his favourite things to eat, including chocolate ice-cream with chocolate chips, but he didn't even feel like eating that.

Nothing made him feel good, not even snuggling up with his lion hot-water bottle cover and putting lion's tufty tail against his nose. Nothing took away the nasty, scratchy, itchy, hot and bothered feeling.

So he wasn't pleased, one Monday morning, when his mum said, 'I've got to go to the dentist, Matthew, but Little Mouse Grandma is coming round to look after you.'

'Why have you got to go to the dentist? Don't go. Stay here. Look after me.' He knew he was being whiny and cross, but he couldn't help it.

His mum said, 'Little Mouse Grandma will look after you, Matthew. You know that.'

'Of course he knows,' said another voice. Little Mouse Grandma! There she was, in his bedroom doorway, with her red safety helmet swinging from one hand and a bulging bag hanging from the other. Matthew couldn't help cheering up a little bit – just to see her.

'Off you go, Alice,' Little Mouse Grandma said to Matthew's mum. 'You'll be late for your appointment if you don't go now. And take that cat with you.'

Ginger Biscuit was sitting on the landing. He was quite a large kitten now. Matthew's mum said she would put him outside. She kissed Matthew behind his ear – she found a space where he hadn't got a spot – then she click-clacked across the wooden floor in her high heels. She stooped down when she reached the landing and picked up Ginger Biscuit.

Matthew couldn't hear her high heels click-clacking down the stairs because of the thick carpet, and he forgot to listen for her closing the door, as he was talking to Little Mouse

Grandma. She was explaining about magic powder. She said she had some in her bag.

'Magic powder! What does it do, Little Mouse Grandma?'

'It magics away itches, Matthew.'

Magic powder! It was just what he wanted.

It was white and it was in a white packet with red and black writing on it.

You had to put it in the bath, Little Mouse Grandma said, and mix it with water. They went into the bathroom and Matthew turned the taps on. Then he sprinkled in the magic powder. Little Mouse Grandma swished it a bit. Then she said a magic rhyme, which she called a spell.

She closed her eyes as she said it:

'By all the powers of Grandma Mouse
Itches! Itches! Leave this house!
Itches! Itches! Go away!
Matthew wants to play today!'

Little Mouse Grandma delved into her bag and brought out a brand-new pair of swimming trunks with dolphins on them. She said she hoped they fitted him, because they were going to play 'At the Sea-side.'

While Matthew tried on the swimming

trunks, Little Mouse Grandma searched in her bag again and brought out some sea shells. She held a big curly one against Matthew's ear. 'Can you hear the sea, Matthew?'

He said he could hear a sighing sound.

'That's the sea,' said Little Mouse Grandma. 'Now jump in!'

The water felt silky smooth. It wasn't hot and it wasn't cold – and it started to take away the itching straight away. Little Mouse Grandma said Matthew must have a long soak to make the

magic work really well. So he lay back in the water and Little Mouse Grandma arranged shells round the edge of the bath. She hung some green-black seaweed on the taps so that Matthew could smell the sea, and she gave him a real sponge to squeeze. 'Real sponges grow in the sea,' she said.

It was all very interesting, but Matthew couldn't help thinking that Little Mouse Grandma had forgotten the most important thing. When was she going to turn into a mouse? He wanted to ask her, though he didn't usually have to. He was about to ask when she looked into her bag again and brought out a boat which she put in the bath. It was a splendid boat. It was blue and white and red and yellow. It had a rudder and a sail and a life-ring and a lift-up deck. It had a fishing rod and five fishes and a hole for a sailor to stand in. In fact it needed only one thing.

'I wish there was a little sailor, Little Mouse Grandma,' Matthew said.

And a voice answered, 'Your wish has come true, Matthew.'

He looked down and there she was – a sailor mouse – on the wet floor beside the bath wearing a sailor hat!

'Where did you get that hat, Little Mouse Grandma?' he asked.

'I got it from a cracker,' she said. 'Lift

me up, Matthew, please.' He lifted her on to the bath rack.

Matthew gazed at her. He gazed at her damp fur, which was a bit wavy now. He gazed at her tiny toes, which he'd never seen so clearly before. Then she said, 'I'd really like to sail, Matthew.'

So he helped her into the boat.

She was just the right size.

He said, 'Where would you like to go, Sailor Mouse?'

She said, 'To the Flannel Islands, please.'

So he blew very gently as she stood on deck and steered.

She went under Bath Rack Pier and round Pumice Stone Rock, till at last she reached the Flannel Islands. There were two of them. One was pink, the other green.

Matthew said, 'Aren't you going to get off here, Little Mouse Grandma?'

She said, 'They're pretty, Matthew, but they don't look safe to me. I think I'll go to Tapland.' She pointed to the taps at the other end of the bath.

He blew again – very gently – and she sailed on and on and on, till at last they reached Tapland.

Matthew said, 'Are you going to get off here, Little Mouse Grandma?'

And she looked up and said, 'I'd like to visit Tapland, Matthew, but I couldn't possibly climb those enormous snowy cliffs. They look very slippery.'

So he said, 'I'll help you, Little Mouse Grandma.' And he did!

Then Little Mouse Grandma stood between the hot tap and the cold tap. She sighed and said, 'Do you know what I've always wanted to do, Matthew?'

'No, Little Mouse Grandma.'

'I've always wanted to water-ski,' she said.

Now, Matthew had seen water-skiers on the telly, on their water skis, whizzing across the water, ever so fast. It did look exciting. Little Mouse Grandma loved to go fast, he knew that, so he said, 'Have you got any water skis, Little Mouse Grandma?'

'No Matthew, I haven't.' And she

sighed such a big sigh that Matthew longed to help her. He looked all around the bathroom. Then he reached over to the rack above the sink for two toothbrushes and some dental floss. Dental floss was a sort of string which his dad used to clean between his teeth.

First he made some loops to keep Little Mouse Grandma's feet on the toothbrush skis. Then he tied two strings of floss to the boat.

'I hope this works,' he said, as he handed the two strings to Little Mouse Grandma.

'I think it might,' she said as she stepped on to the water.

Matthew made the boat whizz, and Little Mouse Grandma whizzed too! To and fro they whizzed, from one end of the bath to the other, with

the water shooting up all around them!

Again and again they did it.

'That was wonderful!' said Little
Mouse Grandma, when at last she'd had
enough skiing and was safely on the side
again. 'Thank you, Matthew. But I really
am soaked now. I had better go and
change.'

When Matthew's mum came home she said, 'You look much better, Matthew. Have you had a nice time?'

He said, 'It was better than nice. It was magic, Mum, thank you very much.' And he told her all about Little Mouse Grandma and the magic powder.

If you enjoyed this

look out for:

Blair the Winner!

Theresa Breslin
Illustrated by *Ken Cox*

It's not fair being in the middle,
like Blair.
Little Baby Willis is a pest.
Big sister Melissa thinks Blair's the pest.
And all the family never stop nagging!

But it's Blair who saves the day
on a camping trip that goes wrong . . .